the mermaid's j... to find her mother

Katherine Langrish

forsaken

"Langrish is a first-rate
storyteller" The Times

Also by Katherine Langrish:

forsaken

Katherine Langrish

EDGE
FRANKLIN WATTS

LONDON•SYDNEY

First published in 2011
by Franklin Watts

Text © Katherine Langrish 2011
Cover design by Peter Scoulding

Franklin Watts
338 Euston Road
London NW1 3BH

Franklin Watts Australia
Level 17/207 Kent Street
Sydney, NSW 2000

A CIP catalogue record for this book
is available from the British Library.

Cover credit: main-Chris A. Crumley/Alamy. c-night-cat/Shutterstock
b/gr –Temmuz Can Arsiray/istockphoto

ISBN: 978 1 4451 0557 4

1 3 5 7 9 10 8 6 4 2

Printed in Great Britain

Franklin Watts is a division of Hachette Children's Books,
an Hachette UK company.
www.hachette.co.uk

*For Liz Kessler, who discovered me
and the trolls, and inspired the mermaids –
with love and splashes.*

Chapter One

Mama had gone.

The house was dark, the baby was crying. Oh, how he cried, long sad wails that would pull the heart from your breast! He was hungry – hungry for warm, rich milk – and how could I feed him? I'm only ten. I dived down across the room and plucked him out of the cradle. I clasped him to my bare chest and wound my long hair around him. I pushed my mouth close to his ear and sang him a hushing song like the ocean in a shell.

Through the gloom of the deep water I could see the rich gleam of the mother-of-pearl cradle we'd all once slept in. Mer-children don't usually have cradles. But then mer-women don't mother their offspring. They have lots of them all at once, like fish. They leave filmy clouds of jellied eggs swaying about in the seaweed; if you look closely you can see hundreds of transparent little curled-up taily things, waiting to hatch. When they start darting about, most of them get eaten by fish. Not one in a hundred survives. Perhaps that's why there aren't very many merfolk, and the ones that do grow up are all a little cold-hearted.

But Mama's different, and we are all proud of her. She had only seven children in eleven years, and all seven of us lived. She looked after each one of us, and taught us to look after the others too. I'm the eldest. My name's Mara.

Father is the Sea-king. It was right that he should have a rare bride, a woman from the land. We all knew how they'd met: she'd been standing at the sea's edge, shading her eyes, when he rose up from the waves and called her along the glittering road the sun makes as it sets over the water. They'd fallen in love at once. And he caught her in his arms and covered her with cold kisses and carried her down – down to our pale palace in the deep.

So of course Mama was special. She had legs, for one thing, though she hid them under clinging silvery dresses that looked almost like our tails. But the most special thing of all about Mama was this: she had a soul.

I can't tell you what a soul is. Even Mama, who had one, could never describe it or say where it was. It's not like your heart which you can feel beating, or your brain that you think with. I don't see the use of a soul, myself, but Mama was firm about it.

She knew that she had one, and she knew that mer-people didn't.

Apparently, it's very important.

My baby brother stopped crying. He was exhausted. I pressed his crumpled face to my shoulder. His hair was as soft and dark as fine weeds. I stroked his tiny back, teasing the long fin on his spine. His mackerel tail beat weakly against the water. He was a prince of the sea, he was half human, and he was dying slowly.

Seven days without milk.

Seven days without Mama.

She'd begged Father for a holiday.

"Let me go back, just for one day, to pray in the little grey church," she'd said. "Isn't it enough that my children have no souls, without losing my own as well?" She looked so terribly sad.

We didn't understand. If she couldn't see her soul, or feel it, how would she ever know whether it was lost or not? But any one of us would have crossed the seven seas for Mama. Her mysterious soul was precious to her, and we all wanted her to keep it.

"It's been eleven years," Mama pleaded. "Let me hear the holy church bells calling me to pray."

How could Father refuse? He trusted her; we all did. So we let Mama go,

and when the long day ended we all
swam together into the warm, cloudy
waters of the bay with bunches of coral
to give to her, and wreaths of shells to
throw around her neck. We watched
and waited for her to come running
home to us over the sand.

She never came.

Chapter Two

The current tugged through the room.
I could sense the tide turning. My family
would soon be home. Every day since
she left, they followed the high tide far
into the bay, calling "Mama!" from the
tops of the tumbling breakers – their
thin voices like seagulls crying. Not me.

I'd had enough of waiting and calling.

I tucked the baby back in the seashell cradle as it rocked gently in the sea sway, anchoring him into his harness of ribbon-weed. I dropped a kiss on his forehead. Then with a slash of my tail I rode the current out of the window. I was furious, with Father as well as with Mama. What was the good of crying and calling from the breakers? How was she ever going to hear? It was pointless: it was feeble.

If I wanted Mama back, I would have to go and fetch her.

I put my arms together over my head and shot upwards. The rugged pinnacles of Father's palace dropped away. I swam fast; I didn't want the others to see me. I whirled through rosy clouds of krill, through a shoal of herring that divided and sprayed around me like a silver fountain. I left the blue deeps, aiming for the round, crinkled, shifting lid that was the light of the world above. Suddenly the water was full of dazzling bubbles. I felt the swells catch and throw me. My head splashed out into the air.

I shut my eyes against the brightness. When I could open them again I saw the land, with a cluster of humans' houses clinging to it like shellfish stuck to a rock, and a bridge over the river, and a white road winding up the hill to a church with a square grey tower.

I sprang high out of the water for a better look. Was Mama still inside, still praying? How much time did praying take anyway?

A harsh metal clanging sound began. *Ring! Ding! Ring! Ding!* In the thin air it hurt my ears. I sank into the waves. It was the bells – the noise Mama wanted to hear for the good of her soul. How could she suffer it?

Hah! But if the bells were ringing, Mama would be in the church for sure. Perhaps I could get closer by swimming up the river. I'd have to be quick, though, with the tide still going out, or I might get stuck on the sandbanks and be left flapping around like a stranded flounder.

The river was bone-cold and noisy, and tasted of mud. Black eels slithered away below me. I thrashed upstream, dodging all sorts of rubbish, rotten wood and tangles of old fishing nets. When the water went cold and dark, and the push of the current got stronger, I knew I was swimming under the bridge. The stone sides were covered with bright green weed an arm's length deep, and the water tasted foul: slime and stone.

I came up on the other side, looking for the church, but the riverbanks and the high stone piers of the bridge closed me in. From above, the bells clanged louder than ever.

Ring, ding; ring, ding; ring, ding.

Ring, ding, dong; ring, ding, dong.

Ring, ding, dong; ring, ding, dong.

I'd come here to call Mama, but no way would she ever hear me over those hateful bells. I tried, though. "Mama! Mama!" But I could hardly hear myself.

I lay finning my tail in the rapid water so as not to be swept away, and tried to think. It panicked me to feel the land so tight and close. I felt trapped in this narrow, smelly river with all its rush and noise. I wanted to turn around right then and go whirling out to sea, back to the rich, dark, hidden rooms of our underwater palace. And then I thought of my baby brother, crying in his cradle. He needed Mama most of all. I couldn't give up.

Against the bridge a flight of grey stone steps ran up from the water. I looked at them in frustration, knowing I couldn't use them. If only I could reach the bridge, I might be able to see the church. Underwater, a flick of the tail would send me gliding up there in moments.

But wait. I'm half human. Was there a chance – even a tiny chance – that, out of water, I might suddenly grow legs?

So I grabbed the bottom step, smacked my tail into the water and boosted myself on to the stones.

All my muscles strained. I nearly

tumbled straight back into the river. My fins sprang open and fanned uselessly against the air. I clung to the steps with my fingertips, and lay there gasping. I pushed my face against the warm stone and peeked down at my tail.

So I wasn't going to grow legs. But now I'd got so far, I was going on. I raised my body on my hands and dragged myself up. I'm light and strong, but my tail is slippery, so when I got tired I lay resting on my front, the hard stone edges digging into me. I tore my hands. I cut my arms. I left slime and silver scales on the edge of every step, but somehow I kept going.

Then the sun came out from behind a cloud.

Underwater, the sun's a blue glow, or at worst a cool white dazzle. Living in the sea, you never get too hot. It's fun to swim in and out of the warm surface water, porpoising up into bright shallows and diving back into cold deeps.

This sun was like something alive and close, blasting me with its fierce breath. Merfolk have moist, thin skin. Soon I would begin to crackle like seaweed left on the beach. I heaved and flopped my way up the steps. Nearly there! The river seemed far, far below. The bells banged on, hammering my ears:

Ring, ding, dong; ring, ding, dong.

Ring, ding, dong.

Ring, ding, dong.

Ring, ding, dong.

Until suddenly they slowed:

Dong...Dong... Dong...

Dong...

Dong...

Dong...

Chapter Three

At the top of the stairs was a gap in
the parapet for people to pass on to the
bridge. I heard voices, and footsteps.
"Hurry, Margaret, or we'll be late." I
stretched over the last few steps, and
with my nose pressed to the stone sill, I
peeped through the gap and saw two

women walk past. Their long skirts swished from side to side – how easy they made it look! Then I saw one of them was Mama.

"No, we mustn't be late," she was saying. "Oh, how wonderful to be going to church again!"

"God has saved you from the perils of the sea," said her friend.

I thrashed my tail on the stones. "Mama!" I tried to call, but my throat was baked dry and it came out as a croak.

She was already out of sight, but I heard the rustle of her skirt pause. "What was that?"

"Only a frog," said her friend. "Hurry!" And they were gone.

A frog! Tears fell from my eyes. All this while, though I'd been angry with Mama for having such a lovely time praying that she'd forgotten to come home, I'd never – no, not once – imagined that she was escaping her life in the sea. Escaping from us!

When I knew that, I humped myself through the gap in the bridge and on to the roadway. I didn't care who saw me, I didn't care if I died trying, I was going to follow Mama into this church where humans saved their invisible souls. I was going to find out what made it more important than us.

Dong...

Dong...

Hand over hand I pulled myself uphill, digging my elbows into the sharp white gravel. My fingers bled and my eyes filled with stinging grey dust. My delicate tail fins became tattered and curled.

Flies buzzed over me like I was something left on the tideline. My back blistered. My elbows stung, and at each heave I scraped more scales off my tail, and the raw places oozed clear lymph, as if my whole body was weeping. Fury and misery kept me going. I swiped my gritty, tangled hair out of my eyes and crawled on.

Dong.

The final note went humming overhead and faded. I rested, gasping.

I was high up the hill now. A warm breeze bent the roadside grasses, carrying a whiff of salt. In the silence left by the bells I could just hear the far-off lullaby of the sea breaking on the shore. Farewell, it seemed to whisper, farewell. And I knew I would never have enough strength to go back.

From the church came a new sound, strange and wonderful, many voices raised together in song. Mama was in there, singing with the others! She had no idea I was out here in the heat and the dust, crawling up the hill – but she ought to know! Why wasn't she thinking about me? Worrying about me? Why didn't she care?

Tears I couldn't spare fell into the dust.

At last I slithered painfully into the cool shadow of the stone porch, which was as dark as a sea cave. The wooden door was slightly open, and the singing was louder than ever. It stirred at my heart: so warm, so true, so different from the cold sea songs of merfolk. I'd cried myself out, but I understood at last what Mama had been missing so much, and terrible fear fell upon me. She was part of this music and I wasn't.

I was a stranger here. I didn't have a soul.

But I wouldn't give up. I curled raw fingers around the edge of the door, and pulled it wider.

High windows glowed red and blue, much prettier than anything in our sea palace. The people inside had their backs turned and didn't notice me, but facing outwards along the walls were stone images of men and women, robed and crowned. What calm, stern faces they had!

The nearest image was of a young warrior with tall white wings like a seagull's. He gazed out over my head,

leaning on his stone sword. The sight
of him made me feel better. Those
beautiful seagull wings belonged to the
ocean, and if the humans didn't mind
his wings, then maybe they wouldn't
mind my tail. Maybe after all they
would welcome me into this place. I
slapped my hands down and squirmed
in over cool, smooth flagstones.

The winged warrior saw me. His
blank stone eyes widened, his stiff stone
feathers ruffled and twitched. He lifted
his white sword and pointed it at me.
He opened his stone mouth gaping
wide and let out a piercing screech of
anger like a sea eagle.

The singing died into a gabble of

screams and cries. A child yelled, "Look, a fish-girl!"

People turned and saw me.

"A mermaid – a soulless mermaid!" someone shouted.

"Turn it out! How did it get here? Turn it out!" someone else cried.

And one after another, with a sound like slow thunder, all the stone images along the walls swivelled, glaring at me, threatening me with staffs and crooks, or hiding their eyes as if even to look at me would be an offence.

On the cold floor I lay shaking; a hateful and rejected thing.

Down from the end of the church strode a stern-looking man in black robes. "Get out! Begone from this holy place!"

Where was Mama? I searched the faces of the crowd staring at me. To them, I was a monster. A filthy, soulless thing crawling on the ground like a lobster. Their looks were killing me. I couldn't breathe. My heart threatened to burst.

Then I saw her. Her hands were pressed to her chest and her eyes were dark with horror. If Mama could look at me like that I must be a monster after all, and I'd never known it. I bowed my head to the ground.

"Mara!" she screamed – and I knew she was still my mother.

They tried to grab her – hold her back – but she wrenched away and threw herself on her knees beside me. "Mara, what are you doing here?"

How stupid parents can be!

I whispered, "I came to find you."

"Your skin! It's all split and sore. What have you done to yourself? You're so dry – so terribly dry!" She gathered me into her arms. It hurt, and I tried not to cry out. "Some of you help me, quickly. We must take her back to the sea."

The man in black stepped forward. "Margaret, beware of her!"

Mama stared at him. "Beware of my own child?"

"Your child?" He gazed at her with shock and pity. Then almost whispering he said, "But she is not a human child, Margaret. She has no soul."

That word again! Mama's head jerked back. With an effort she got to her feet and I clung to her neck, writhing my sore tail around her. She carried me to the church door.

"Stop, Margaret!" the man cried.

"She has no soul, and whether she dies today or a hundred years from now, she will vanish like a little wreath of salt foam on the beach. But when you die, your soul will live for ever. Do not go with her, Margaret."

I felt Mama shudder, but hugging me close, she turned and faced him. "Maybe she doesn't have a soul but she is still my daughter!" she told him in a strong voice, though her tears dropped on me. "Besides, isn't she God's creature too? Didn't He make the sea as well as the land? How would I deserve heaven if I left her?"

The man stared at her, while the crowd murmured and fidgeted. I saw him flush. Then he nodded, just a little dip of the head, but it was enough.

Mama pushed backwards through the heavy door, and he didn't follow. As we hurried down the white road in the heat, the singing started up behind us. "O you seas and floods, bless the Lord," they sang. "O you whales and all that move in the waters, bless the Lord: praise him, and magnify him for ever."

I'll never understand humans. Not even Mama.

I was heavy for Mama to carry, I think, because she kept stumbling and muttering. I tightened my grip around her neck. She glanced down at me.

"And you came to find me, all by

yourself? Are you very angry with me, Mara?"

There was too much to say. I thought of my poor little brother, how we'd longed for her, how unhappy we'd been. Then I remembered what the man in the church had said, and hope rose in me.

"Have you lost your soul now, Mama? Did you leave it in the church? Please don't go back for it, Mama. Stay with us always, in the lovely, cool sea."

"The lovely, cool sea," she repeated, and I saw tears in her eyes. "Mara, I was wrong — I was very wrong to leave you."

Though I hurt all over, I was triumphant. How Father would smile, how the little ones would jump like dolphins to see us coming home!

Under her breath she whispered, "*Though I live in the uttermost deeps of the sea, His love shall find me.*"

From the
author

The idea for forsaken
came from a poem called
"The Forsaken Merman"
by a Victorian poet called Matthew Arnold (1822–
1888). Based on an old legend, it tells the story of a
merman who marries a human woman, Margaret.
They live happily together under the sea, until
one day she hears church bells ringing and feels a
sudden longing to go and pray. The merman agrees
to part with her for a short visit. But once on land,
she never returns to the sea, leaving her husband and
little mer-children grieving.

The old belief about mermaids was that – unlike
human beings – they had no souls and therefore no
life after death. Margaret fears she too will lose her
chance of eternal life in heaven if she stays with the
merman under the sea.

But this fear leads her to abandon her husband and children. Was she right to follow her beliefs? Or was she wrong to cause her family such suffering?

In the original Danish legend, the merman clambers into the churchyard to find his wife, but when he peeps into the church, all the little stone statues of saints and angels turn their backs on him.

When I read this, a shiver ran right down my spine, and I knew I had to tell the story again – but this time I wondered what would have happened if, instead of the merman, one of Margaret's own mer-children came to find her?

www.katherinelangrish.co.uk

Get in touch with Katherine through her website, Facebook (https://www.facebook.com/pages/Katherine-Langrish-Author/113662331978121?ref=ts) or Twitter (twitter.com/KathLangrish)

ANDY BRIGGS

WARRIOR NUMBER ONE

EDGE

From the author of HERO.COM and Tarzan: The Greystoke Legacy

A voice in the darkness woke Carl. His first thought was that he was dreaming or that he'd left on the TV. His hand groped for his glasses. Putting them on, he fumbled for the bedside lamp. It clicked uselessly. Had the bulb blown?

Then he noticed a very tall figure at the end of his bed, silhouetted by the streetlight outside. Must be his stupid sister.

"Do you know what time it is?" he mumbled.

"It is time to rise and meet your fate, Warrior!"

Carl sat bolt upright – that wasn't his sister unless something had seriously gone wrong. The voice sounded like the narrator from *Barbarianz*.

"W–who are you?"

As the darkness moved, Carl caught sight of a long cape that stretched into the TV screen.

"Folks call me the Sheriff. I've sought this world for you!"

Carl heard a horse whinny and, as his eyes adjusted, he could see the shape of a horse beneath the figure. Carl relaxed slightly; the animal confirmed that he must be dreaming. It would be impossible to get a horse up the stairs without his mum raising a fuss.

"Why me?"

"Are you not Warrior Number One?" Carl shoved his glasses back up his nose and nodded. "Then join me!

Castellian has need of you! Rise, Warrior King!" boomed the man.

A cold leather glove snapped around Carl's hand and hoisted him onto the back of the horse.

The horse reared onto two legs. Carl threw his hands around the Sheriff's waist so he didn't slip off. The horse spun around and galloped towards the TV. Carl braced for impact – but instead his ears popped as the LED screen stretched like rubber and they passed through with a brief whiff of electrified air.

The horse's footfalls echoed as they passed through a tunnel. Seconds later they emerged, and Carl hiccupped in shock at what he saw—

They were in a sunlit vista of rolling forest-covered hills. Jagged snow-capped mountains crowned the horizon, mirrored in a huge lake that stretched to the foot of the trees.

The landscape passed in a blur. For several minutes the Sheriff said nothing. They trotted into an idyllic glade and the horse stooped to drink from a cascading waterfall. Carl took his cue to slide from its back. It was a long way down. Soft moss cushioned his landing, but he still managed to clumsily twist his ankle. The air was heavily scented and was rich with pollen, which triggered Carl's hay fever. How could this be a dream?

Want to find out what happens to Carl? Get hold of a copy of Warrior Number One today!